First published 2005 by Walker Books Ltd
87 Vauxhall Walk, London SE11 5HJ

This edition published 2007

8 10 9 7

© 2005 Lucy Cousins

Lucy Cousins font © 2005 Lucy Cousins

The right of Lucy Cousins to be identified as the author/illustrator of this
work has been asserted by her in accordance with the Copyright,
Designs and Patents Act 1988

Illustrated in the style of Lucy Cousins by King Rollo Films Ltd
"Maisy" Audio Visual Series produced by King Rollo Films Ltd
for Universal Pictures International Visual Programming

Maisy™. Maisy is a registered trademark of Walker Books Ltd, London.

Printed in China

British Library Cataloguing in Publication Data:
a catalogue record for this book is
available from the British Library

ISBN 978-1-4063-0696-5

www.walker.co.uk

Maisy Goes
to the Library

Lucy Cousins

WALKER BOOKS
AND SUBSIDIARIES

LONDON • BOSTON • SYDNEY • AUCKLAND

Maisy likes going to the library.

How lovely to look at a book in a nice quiet place.

It was the sort of day when Maisy wanted a book about fish.

She found a flappy book about birds ... but no fish.

She found a shiny green book about turtles ...

and a great big stripy book about tigers... but no fish!

Never mind, there are so many other things to do in the library...

make a
copy of your
favourite
picture...

look at the
fish in the
aquarium...

Aquarium?

That's it! So Maisy looked
by the aquarium...

and that's exactly where
she found a book about fish...
and it was sparkly!

Maisy settled down
to read in a quiet corner.

But then Cyril and
Tallulah came along...

and started
laughing (at Tallulah's
funny face!).

And then Eddie
came in ...

and shouted "Story time!"

because Ostrich was going to tell a story in the Story corner...

Maisy's quiet corner!

charley sturted luughing.

"She swallowed a dog to catch the cat!"

Then everyone started laughing!

Woof-woof!

And they were still laughing when they checked out their books,

and went outside
to play.

In the park, Cyril and Charley pretended to be the old woman and her dog.

Woof-woof!

Tallulah meowed like a cat...and
Eddie neighed like a horse.

Meeow!   And Maisy...?

Neigh!

Maisy read
her sparkly book
about fish in a
nice ... quiet ...
place ...